"White, No. Pink, Yes," Casey Announced.

"What did you say?" Jake asked.

"White, no. Pink, yes."

Casey's eyes were fixed on the plastic stick in front of her as if it meant life or death. Irritation simmered inside him. He glanced around the room, looking for clues. Suddenly his gaze landed on an unfolded set of instructions lying half in the sink. Frowning, he reached for them at the same moment she spoke again.

"Since it's pink, do you suppose that means it's a girl? No," she continued, "pink just means pregnant. It could be a boy."

Girl? Boy? Jake's mouth went dry and his brain blanked out. Was she saying what he thought she was saying? No. Of course not.

But when she lifted her head and met his gaze through wide teary eyes, he knew it was true.

"Congratulations, Jake. We're pregnant...."

Dear Reader,

Happy Holidays to all of you from the staff of Silhouette Desire! Our celebration of Desire's fifteenth anniversary continues, and to kick off this holiday season, we have a wonderful new book from Dixie Browning called *Look What the Stork Brought*. Dixie, who is truly a Desire star, has written over sixty titles for Silhouette.

Next up, *The Surprise Christmas Bride* by Maureen Child. If you like stories chock-full of love and laughter, this is the book for you. And Anne Eames continues her MONTANA MALONES miniseries with *The Best Little Joeville Christmas*.

The month is completed with more Christmas treats: *A Husband in Her Stocking* by Christine Pacheco; *I Married a Prince* by Kathryn Jensen and *Santa Cowboy* by Barbara McMahon.

I hope you all enjoy your holidays, and hope that Silhouette Desire will add to the warmth of the season. So enjoy the very best in romance from Desire!

Melissa Senate

Senior Editor

Please address questions and book requests to:
Silhouette Reader Service
U.S.: 3010 Walden Ave., P.O. Box 1325, Buffalo, NY 14269
Canadian: P.O. Box 609, Fort Erie, Ont. L2A 5X3

MAUREEN CHILD

THE SURPRISE CHRISTMAS BRIDE

SILHOUETTE *Desire*

Published by Silhouette Books

America's Publisher of Contemporary Romance

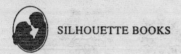

SILHOUETTE BOOKS

ISBN 0-373-76112-0

THE SURPRISE CHRISTMAS BRIDE

Printed in U.S.A.

Books by Maureen Child

Silhouette Desire

Have Bride, Need Groom #1059
The Surprise Christmas Bride #1112

MAUREEN CHILD

was born and raised in Southern California and is the only person she knows who longs for an occasional change of season. She is delighted to be writing for Silhouette and is especially excited to be a part of the Desire line.

An avid reader, she looks forward to those rare, rainy California days when she can curl up and sink into a good book. Or two. When she isn't busy writing, she and her husband of twenty-five years like to travel, leaving their two grown children in charge of the neurotic golden retriever who is the *real* head of the household. She is also an award-winning historical writer under the names Kathleen Kane and Ann Carberry.

To the gang at Sunshine Books:
Nita, Betty and Ron.
You guys are the best.

One

"Maybe I should put the top up before I drown."

Casey Oakes pushed wet hair out of her eyes and squinted into the freezing rain. A deep hard shiver rippled through her. "Too late now to bother," she grumbled, and told herself that maybe it would be a blessing if she *did* drown. At least then she would have done something no other Oakes had ever managed. Drowning in a convertible while cruising the back roads outside Simpson, California, wasn't, as her mother would say, "what society expects of an Oakes."

Accomplishing that feat in a wedding gown would only add to the myth, she told herself. A few years from now, her little ride would probably become the stuff of local folklore. People would tell the story of Cassandra Oakes in hushed tones around campfires.

Parents would discipline misbehaving children with the threat of a nighttime visit from the Drowned Bride.

Still smiling to herself, Casey flinched when her soggy veil flew in front of her face and blocked her view of the road. She slammed on the brakes, heard something under her car snap, then came to a shuddering halt.

She cut the engine, and when that powerful noise disappeared, all that was left was the sound of the heavy rain pelting on and all around her. The windshield wipers continued to slap rhythmically as they futilely tried to do battle with the downpour. Nearly an inch of water covered the floorboards, no doubt ruining the plush scarlet carpet. Casey winced as she realized that the leather seats probably weren't faring any better.

"Well, hell," she muttered to no one, "who expected rain?" But then, with the way the rest of her day had gone, why *not* rain? Heck, why not a blizzard?

Reaching up, she pushed her veil to the back of her head and looked around at the drenched countryside. The road wasn't much more than a narrow dirt track, covered yearly by a thin layer of gravel. Now the ground-up rock was practically floating atop a sea of churning mud. On either side of the road wooden fence posts, strung with barbed wire, stood at attention for miles. Behind those fences lay open ground. Meadow grasses, waving and dipping with the wind and rain, a few gnarled leafless trees that looked as though they'd been there for centuries, a veritable forest of giant pines, their needles dipping with the weight of the rain—and that was it.

No houses.

No lights.

No people.

To top it all off, it had been so long since she'd been back in Simpson she didn't know if she was close to the Parrish ranch or not.

Casey inhaled sharply and felt the familiar sting of tears filling her eyes. Roughly she brushed them away with the backs of her hands.

She already had all the water she could handle.

Then she heard it.

The call came softly at first, then built into a low throbbing moan.

Frowning, Casey stepped out of the car and grimaced as the cold mud oozed over the tops of her white satin pumps. When her right foot slid out from under her in the muck, she forgot all about her ruined shoes. She grabbed at the car door for balance and managed somehow to keep from landing facedown in the thick brown river at her feet.

"Yuck." A sucking noise accompanied the movement as she lifted one shoeless foot from the icy mud. She heard the moaning sound again and turned her head to find the source.

Her eyes widened and a rush of sympathy for something besides herself washed over her.

"Oh, you poor little thing," she crooned, and started slogging through the mud.

"No, I don't want to tell you what it is." Jake Parrish laughed, shook his head and reached for his coffee cup. His sister, Annie, hadn't changed a bit over the years. Grown-up or not, she still couldn't stand suspense.

"C'mon Jake," she pleaded over the phone. "One little hint. Just one."

"Nope," he told her, and took a sip of coffee. "You'll just have to get out here first thing in the morning if you want your curiosity satisfied."

"You really are an evil man, big brother."

"Yeah, I know." He grinned, then added, "Oh, and would you mind bringing Dad, Uncle Harry and Aunt Emma, too?"

Annie sucked in a gulp of air and Jake could almost see his younger sister's black eyebrows shooting into her hairline. Lord, how she hated not knowing everything.

"This must be big," she finally said.

"Big enough," Jake assured her.

"Dammit, Jake!" Annie's voice dropped into the stern no-nonsense tone she used on her three-year-old, Lisa. "You know I hate surprises. If you don't give me something to go on, I won't get a wink of sleep all night."

She wouldn't, either. Memories rushed through him. The night before her birthday, Annie would lie awake all night, wondering what she might receive. And Christmas Eve was even worse. Then she was so bad not only did *she* stay awake, she kept Jake up, too.

"All right," he said with a smile. "One little hint."

"Yesss!"

Jake frowned thoughtfully as he tried to figure out a way to phrase the hint without giving away too much of his surprise. He leaned back against the kitchen wall, crossed his feet at the ankles and stared up at the overhead light fixture. Shaped like a wagon wheel, the chandelier held six globe-covered lightbulbs, which shone brightly against the late-afternoon gloom.

He shifted his gaze to the storm raging outside the window. Thanks to the deal he'd just managed to pull off, he told himself, not even the torrential rain or predicted snow could ruin his good mood.

"Jake..."

"Oh! Sorry, Annie. Just thinkin'."

"Don't strain yourself."

"Very funny. Maybe I won't give you that hint, after all."

"Jake Parrish, if you don't..."

He laughed and pushed away from the wall. "OK, you win. Here's your hint. It's something I've wanted for a long time."

A lengthy silent pause. Then, "that's *it?*" Outrage colored her voice.

"That's it. Until tomorrow."

"I said it before and I'll say it again. You're an evil man, Jake. And you're going to hell."

"Probably. But that's all right. At least all of my friends will be there with me."

"Count on it."

In answer he gave her a deep-throated malevolent chuckle. He wasn't surprised to hear her hang up in disgust.

Oh, he knew his little sister would find a way to make him pay for dragging this out. But dammit, it would be worth it. He'd waited a long time for this. And he wanted to enjoy every minute of it.

He hung up the phone, walked across the room to the gray granite countertop and set his coffee cup down. Then he leaned forward to peer through the rain-spattered glass at the growing darkness. This was just the beginning, he told himself.

With the conclusion of this deal, his long-held plans for the Parrish ranch were complete at last. Now he could focus on the horse-breeding program he'd been thinking about for months.

Anything was possible.

A slow grin tipped up one corner of his mouth as he took a quick look around the kitchen. Modern appliances, a gleaming Spanish-tile floor and a kiva-shaped fireplace in the corner made the kitchen something of a showplace. Not that he could do anything more complicated than a pot of coffee, grilled cheese sandwiches and an assortment of microwavable delights.

That didn't matter, though. For Jake had made good on his promises. He had turned the ranch into a business prosperous enough to pay off all the cosmetic changes to the house that his ex-wife had insisted on. And despite Linda's efforts, she hadn't managed to empty his pockets.

Jake frowned slightly at the memory of the woman he had allowed to make a fool of him, but then he dismissed all thoughts of her. Instead, he concentrated on the ranch. His accomplishment. His triumph. The place was now a far cry from how it had looked while he and Annie had been growing up.

In his mind's eye he could still see the antique stove his mother had somehow coaxed into working long beyond the time it should have. If he tried hard enough, he could make out the shadow of the battered pine table where he and then Annie had done their schoolwork. The same table where the family had gathered at suppertime for loud long discussions on everything from the Chicago Cubs to Darwin.

Jake blinked, and in place of that old familiar table was the heavy Santa Fe style polished-oak dining set Linda had purchased three years before. He frowned thoughtfully. True, the ranch hadn't had much in the way of comforts when he was a kid. But there was always enough love.

The one thing his new and improved ranch house lacked.

Jake shook his head and reached for his coffee cup. He took one last drink of the still-hot brew, then slammed the cup back down onto the counter. Keep your mind on business, he told himself. Thoughts of love and what-might-have-beens wouldn't get his work done.

And thoughts of Linda would only give him an ulcer.

"Besides," he said aloud into the empty room, "you've got to check the fencing before nightfall." With the rain and the howling wind, he couldn't risk wires coming down and his stock wandering out onto the roads.

Besides, if the weatherman was right for a change

and the first snow of the season was really headed in that night, then he'd best keep ahead of the chores.

He snatched his rain slicker and hat from the pegs near the back door and pulled them on, purposely keeping his back to the shiny sterile room. The sooner he was started, the sooner he'd be back. With a microwaved pizza, a beer and a front-row seat for the football game on TV.

If he kept the volume loud enough, he just might be able to convince himself that he wasn't really lonely.

"I know just how you feel," Casey told the little animal, and reached down to grab another handful of wet white lace. Draping the fabric across the calf's shivering body, she hovered over him, blocking most of the rain with her back. She stroked his neck and looked into his sad brown eyes. "It's no fun being cold and wet and alone, is it, pal?"

The calf snorted.

"Gesundheit," Casey said automatically, then blew fruitlessly at a sopping-wet lock of blond hair hanging in front of her right eye. She didn't want to let go of the calf long enough to shove her hair and what was left of her veil off her face. The poor little thing was so scared it would probably take off, and she'd never manage to catch it again, running in the mud.

The trembling calf shifted position, leaning into her. She staggered under its surprising weight and looked back into those big brown eyes. "Do you know something? Your eyes are a lot like my fiancé's. Or rather, my ex-fiancé's.'' She frowned slightly before adding, ''But don't worry, I won't hold that against you. They look better on you, anyway.''

The animal snorted and bawled again.

''I felt like crying myself earlier,'' she murmured sympathetically. ''You might not know this, but I was supposed to get married today.''

Her little friend shivered heavily.

''I know. It gives me cold chills just to think about it now.'' Casey leaned down and rubbed her cheek against the back of the animal's head. Her feet felt like two blocks of muddy ice and she was beginning to lose feeling in her fingers altogether. Stupid weather. Trying to ignore her own discomfort, she kept talking to her little friend. ''The worst part was telling everyone that there wouldn't be a wedding. You should have seen their faces, pal.''

He mooed quietly.

''Who?'' she asked with a choked laugh. ''The people in the church, of course.'' She sniffed. ''And my parents. It's a good thing for Steven that his note said he was going to Mexico. If my father had been able to get his hands on that jerk…'' She sighed and lifted her head to look at her new friend again. ''It's not every day a girl gets jilted, you know. Don't you think I should be feeling worse than I am about all this?''

The calf shook its head.

''I don't, either,'' Casey's fingers stroked the animal's rough yet smooth hide. She shivered hard before saying, ''Now don't be offended because I said your eyes were like Steven's. It's not your fault, after all. Besides," she pointed out with a wry smile, "you seem to have a much more pleasant personality."

The calf moved and stomped on her toes.

She yelped and dragged her foot out from under the animal's hoof. "You dance like Steven, too."

The wind kicked up, snatching at her veil and flinging it out around her. "I know it's hard to believe now," she told the squirming calf, "but a few hours ago, I looked pretty good."

An image leaped in her brain. Of her, standing at the back of the church, waiting for her cue to start down the incredibly long pine-bough-decorated aisle at her father's side. She'd looked at her ten maids of honor lined up in front of her and realized she didn't really *know* any of them.

Oh, they went to the same functions. Told the same stories. Laughed at the same jokes. But not one of those ten women would she have considered a friend. Then it had struck her that the one real friend she had wasn't even attending her wedding. Annie had refused to watch her friend make what she called a "giant mistake."

The doubts she'd been battling for months had risen in her again. But then the organ music had started, swelling out into the church and stealing away her breath. The first bridesmaid had been about to start her staggered walk down the aisle when an usher had brought Casey the note from Steven.

During the next few interminably long minutes, she'd endured curious stares, hushed whispers and even a muffled laugh or two. She hadn't been able to find a friendly face anywhere in the crowd of surprised disappointed guests.

Even her parents had been too stunned to offer comfort to her. Her father, grim-faced and tight-lipped, stood awkwardly patting her mother's shoulder as she wept quietly into her hanky. The twins, Casey's older brothers, looked as though they just wanted to find someone to punch.

Naturally, when she ran out of the church a few minutes later and jumped into her sports car—which one of her brothers had thoughtfully driven to the church—she'd instinctively headed for her one real friend.

The only person she could count on to listen to her. To tell her that she wasn't crazy. That she was right to feel as though she'd just escaped from prison.

Annie Parrish.

Casey yanked her full skirt a little higher over the animal's back and told herself that all she had to do now was find the Parrish ranch. Hopefully before she froze to death. It had been only five years since her family had moved out of Simpson. Why did everything look so different?

The rain, she thought. She was only disoriented because of the rain. When the storm passed, she would find the ranch. *If* the storm passed, her mind added silently. She glanced up at the black clouds overhead, noted the wind-whipped trees surrounding the meadow and fought down her first thread of worry. For all she knew, it could start snowing any minute. By morning she would be nothing more than the ice statue of a haggard-looking bride.

The Irish lace and ivory silk dress she wore felt as though it weighed five hundred pounds. The fabric had soaked up the rain like a dime-store sponge, and the heavy mud along the hemline wasn't helping the situation any. Idly she wondered what the gown's designer would say if she could see her creation now.

The world's most expensive tent for water-logged calves.

And what, Casey asked herself, would her father say?

She groaned quietly and closed her eyes for a second or two. Henderson Oakes wasn't going to be a happy man for quite a while. No doubt he would take Casey's being jilted as a personal affront. Though basically good people, her parents were far more concerned about how things looked than with how things really were.

Better not to even think about them yet.

The rain came down harder and began to feel like a thousand cold knives stabbing her body. Her back ached from hunching over the calf. Her arms were scratched from clawing her way through barbed wire to rescue the little beast. She'd lost one shoe to the muck and she definitely felt a cold coming on.

With any luck it would develop into pneumonia.

"Here comes the bride," she sang softly, then stopped abruptly. If she wasn't so blasted tired and if she wasn't afraid she'd sink neck deep in mud, Casey would have plopped right down on the ground and had a good cry.

"What in *hell* are you doing, lady?"

The deep gravelly voice seemed to come out of

nowhere. She jumped, staggered and fell across the calf's sturdy little body. Throwing one hand down onto the muddy ground, Casey broke her fall and ignored the tiny twinge of pain that shot through her wrist. She cocked her head to one side and looked through her veil's saturated netting at a man on a horse.

Finally. Help.

At least she hoped it was help.

She really had to start paying more attention to her surroundings. She'd been so wrapped up in her own thoughts she hadn't even heard the horse and rider approach.

Pushing herself upright, Casey kept one hand on the calf and looked at the man carefully. His hat was pulled down low on his forehead, and an olive green rain slicker covered the rest of him, except for his lower legs and the worn boots shoved into stirrups.

The rain continued to pound relentlessly around them and Casey lifted one hand to shield her eyes, hoping for a better look at the cowboy.

"Cassandra Oakes," he muttered. "I don't believe it."

The obvious displeasure in his tone struck a chord of memory within Casey. How many times had she heard that same raspy voice say, "Get the hell away from me!"? And how many of her dreams had that same raspy voice invaded?

Goosebumps that had nothing to do with the rain and the cold suddenly leaped up on Casey's arms, then raced across her shoulders and down her spine.

Only one man could have such an effect on her.

Even if it *had* been five years since she'd seen him.

Five years since he'd broken her heart.

"Hello, Jake."

Two

Hello, Jake?

That was all she could say? Standing in the middle of his field in a soaking-wet wedding gown, hovering over a mewling calf, and she says, "Hello, Jake"?

A groan rattled through him. When Jake had spotted that convertible on the side of the road, he'd figured someone was in trouble. That road only led to his and Don Wilson's ranches, so there never was much traffic on it. Jake had expected to find some tourist lost in the storm or someone on their way to Don's place.

He sure hadn't expected a bride.

Let alone this *particular* bride.

Man, a day could really go to crap in a hurry, he told himself. Not twenty minutes ago he'd been feeling great. He should have known it wouldn't last.

But dammit, he never would have guessed that it would be *Casey* showing up out of nowhere just in time to ruin his good mood.

Ruefully, though, he admitted that her appearance did make a sort of karmic sense. He mentally bowed to the inevitable and asked, "What the hell are you doing here, Casey?" His gaze swept over her ruined bridal gown quickly. "Looking for a church, are we?"

"Running *from* a church, actually."

"Uh-huh." He leaned forward in the saddle. "And where'd you bury the groom?"

"It's a long story." Her face paled a bit.

"Naturally."

Tipping her head back, she managed to swing her soggy veil out of her face long enough to look at him. Those green eyes of hers locked onto him, and Jake felt his insides tighten into knots.

"I'll tell you all about it later," she said stiffly. "But right now, would you mind helping me?"

No one should be able to look that good covered in mud, he thought absently. Then when desire began to rear its ugly head, he heard himself ask gruffly, "Help you what?"

"Save him." She wagged her head at the calf still cradled in her arms.

No animal had looked less in need of saving. In fact, Jake admitted silently, he wouldn't mind trading places with the damn thing. But he remembered clearly that even years ago, she'd had a soft heart for animals. He chuckled slightly as he recalled the year she'd realized hamburgers actually came from cows.

She'd been horrified. Probably came from living in town all her life. Hell, the only time she or her brothers ever even saw an animal up close was when they came out to the ranch. Their parents had never allowed their children to have a pet of any kind.

Her brothers. Jeez, it had been a long time since Jake had seen the twins. Of course, between working twenty-five hours a day on the ranch and his brief but memorable marriage to Linda, he hadn't had time for any of his old friends.

"Jake? Earth to Jake."

"Huh?" He frowned and forced himself back to the problem at hand. "Oh, yeah. The calf. Save him from what?" He was too wet and cold and tired to be dealing with this. He'd learned long ago that when talking to Casey, it paid to stay alert. Even then, it often wasn't enough.

"He's scared," she said.

"Scared?" Jake's fingers tightened on the reins. Knowing he would regret it, Jake heard himself ask a question, anyway. "And just what is he scared of?"

"The storm, of course."

The wind howled through the trees as if to underline her statement, and the calf squirmed against her. Casey's eyebrows lifted and she nodded shortly as if to say, "See?"

Jake's teeth ground together. She was as stubborn as ever. And as beautiful, his brain added, even with her hair hanging in limp soggy strands along her cheeks. Even with her wedding dress splotched with mud. Even with her emerald eyes squinted against the downpour. Uneasily Jake watched her widen her stance and wiggle her behind as she struggled to get a better grip on the animal.

Something hard and tight settled in his chest, wrapping itself around his lungs and heart. He struggled to draw a breath. Even after five years she still had the same old effect on him.

For the first time since leaving the ranch house, he was beginning to wish his Jeep wasn't out of commission. At least then he'd be seated on a nice comfy bucket seat, instead of futilely trying to find a comfortable position in the saddle. Dammit. He'd always enjoyed riding in the rain.

Until now.

Immediately he told himself to get a grip. She was wearing a damned wedding gown. She'd said she was running from a church. But she hadn't said whether she'd started running before or *after* the wedding.

The notion of Casey's being someone else's wife tightened that cold band around his chest another notch.

Rain pelted his hat and slicker. He felt the slap of each drop and welcomed it. At least he knew what to do about rain. *She* was another matter entirely.

"Are you going to climb down and help me or not?"

Jake shook his head, tightened his grip on the reins with one hand and rubbed his jaw viciously with the other. There was no way he'd be able to climb down from his horse and walk. Even if his rain slicker did hide his body's reaction to her, his discomfort would be all too visible.

But he had to do something.

This ridiculous conversation was getting them nowhere.

"Cows *live* outside," he said.

The calf bawled piteously.

Casey cooed in sympathy, then flashed Jake a hard look. "He's just a baby."

"Who weighs more than you do."

A deep reverberating sound rolled out around them and Casey half straightened, still keeping her arms around the animal beside her.

"What was that?"

"That would be his mama, I'd bet," Jake told her when she swiveled her head to look at him.

The calf called a quavering answer and its mother mooed back.

"Here she comes," Jake said, and dipped his head toward the distant line of trees.

She looked in the direction he indicated and sucked in a quick breath. Mama indeed. A huge cow was lumbering toward her, moving much more quickly than Casey would have thought possible. Apparently her friend didn't need saving as much as *she* did at the moment. Immediately she released the calf and started for the man and relative safety.

She grabbed up fistfuls of skirt, hiked the hem past her knees and trudged through the mud. The cow's hoofbeats pounded against the sodden ground and sounded like native war drums to Casey. It seemed to take forever to cross the few feet of space separating her from the horse, and naturally Jake wasn't offering the slightest bit of help.

Just as that thought raced through her mind, though, he urged his mount closer, kicked free of a stirrup and held out one hand to her.

She looked up at him and didn't see even the tiniest flicker of welcome in his blue eyes. She hesitated, glanced over her shoulder at the approaching two tons of offended motherhood and chose the lesser of two evils.

Slapping her hand into his, she felt his long callused fingers fold around hers in a firm grip. Ignoring the warm tingle of awareness sparking between them, she stuffed one muddied stockinged foot into the stirrup and allowed him to pull her up behind him on the saddle.

Immediately Jake turned his horse around and kneed it into a fast walk. After a few feet he pulled back on the reins, bringing the horse to a stop. He turned in the saddle to look behind him, and she shifted to follow his gaze.

She smiled as she watched the calf dip its head below its mother's belly and nuzzle around for milk. Of course, the cow still didn't look very happy with the two interfering humans, but at least Casey's young friend was safe.

And so was she.

"Here," Jake said, and dropped his hat onto her head.

She tipped the brim back and looked at him.

Rain flattened his thick black hair to his skull, and he reached up to brush it out of his way. His blue eyes were hard as he stared at her, but there was a spark of something else there, as well. Then in a heartbeat it was gone.

"I'll take you to your car."

"Don't bother," she told him, remembering that loud snap when she'd stomped on the brakes. "I think it's broken down."

"Perfect," Jake grumbled, and turned the horse's head. "Wrap your arms around my waist," he said. "It's about a ten-minute ride to the ranch from here."

"What about my car?" She pointed at the abandoned convertible.

Jake frowned and spared the car a quick glance. "We can call for a tow from the house."

When the big animal beneath her jumped into a canter, she jolted backward into nothingness. Quickly she reached for Jake and folded her arms around his hard flat stomach. Scooting in closer to him, she pressed herself against his back and felt his muscles bunch beneath her touch. A warm curl of something she hadn't allowed herself to think about in five years began to thread its way through her body. She squeezed her eyes shut. She'd thought those feelings were gone forever. Lord knew, she'd worked hard at forgetting them.

But apparently she hadn't worked hard enough. Here she was, less than ten minutes with the man, and her knees had turned to rubber. Maybe what she should do was dredge up that memory of the last time she'd seen him. Remember the embarrassment. The humiliation. Surely that would be enough to quell whatever lingering feelings she had for the man.

No. Immediately her mind rejected the plan. She wasn't going to relive that night again. Not for any reason. Not if she could help it, anyway. Besides, she told herself, her reaction to Jake no doubt had more to do with her already emotional state than with the man himself.

She was so cold. So tired. She thought about resting her head on his back, but then reconsidered. No sense racing out to meet problems with open arms.

Deliberately she sat up straight and loosened her hold on his waist a bit. Instead of letting her mind wander down dangerous paths, she concentrated on moving with the familiar rhythm of the horse's steps. Years of riding lessons at exclusive stables were finally paying off.

Jake sucked in a gulp of air and she thought he muttered something.

She shifted to one side, tipped her head back and asked, "What did you say?"

"Nothing," he snapped. "And sit still, will you?"

He dropped her off at the back door to the house, then took his horse to the barn. In no hurry to join the woman waiting in the kitchen, he took his time in unsaddling his mount and drying him off. Only when the horse had been fed, watered and put away for the night did he step to the open doorway and look across the open ground at the house.

Bright light spilled out of the windows, layering the ground's puddled water with brilliant splashes of color. He turned his head to look at the guest house, two hundred yards away. The lights there were off but for a single lamp left burning in what he knew was the living room. The blue Ford pickup was gone from the front of the house.

So, the foreman and his wife had gone into town despite the storm.

That left him and Casey entirely too alone for comfort.

And he couldn't get rid of her anytime soon, either. With his Jeep not working and the pickup gone for who knew how long, they were stuck together.

Dammit, why did she have to show up here? And why was she still able to take his breath away with a single glance?

Grumbling at his own foolishness, he stepped out of the barn, shut the double doors behind him and walked into the wind and rain. He crossed the yard slowly, as if hoping the cold would erase the spark of heat she'd created when she'd wrapped her arms around him. But it didn't help. The fire in his blood remained, and as he recalled the feel of her legs pressed along his own, his body tightened uncomfortably. Halfway to the house, he stopped dead and tilted his head back to glare at the stormy sky.

Hard heavy rain pummeled his face and chest. A cold fierce wind rushed around him, tugging at his coat with frigid fingers. He squinted against the icy pellets and noticed an occasional spot of feathery white drifting down toward him.

Perfect.

Snow.

"What did I ever do to you?" he demanded hoarsely of a silent heaven.

The snowflakes thickened amidst the raindrops.

Jake straightened, shook his head, then loped across the muddy ground to the back porch. He stripped off his slicker and snapped it in the air, shaking off most of the water. Then he dropped it onto the closest chair, stomped the mud from his boots and opened the door to meet trouble face-to-face.

She was standing in front of the kiva fireplace staring into the flames still dancing across the logs he'd laid earlier in the afternoon.

"You're shivering," he said lamely, and she turned to look at him.

"I'm warmer than I was."

Maybe. But her teeth were chattering. His gaze swept over the sodden once-beautiful white dress, and he wondered again about the mysteriously missing groom. What kind of idiot would let a woman like this escape him at his own wedding?

Wet fabric clung to her like a determined lover, outlining her small breasts and the curve of her hips. What should have been a full skirt now hung straight down her legs, wrapping her in a blanket of muddy lace.

A sharp pain pierced his chest as he let himself actually think about her being married to someone else. But in the next instant he buried the pain. What was done was done. He'd made his decision five years ago and he still believed it had been the right one.

No matter *what* it had cost him.

He lifted his gaze to hers, pushed both hands through his wet hair and said gruffly, "What are you doing here, Casey?"

She sniffed, snatched her veil from her head and twisted it between her hands. Dirty water streamed from the sodden netting. "I came to see Annie."

"Oh." His sister. He nodded. Of course she was there to see Annie, you idiot. Why in hell would she have come to see *him?* He inhaled deeply, blew the air out of his lungs with a rush and said, "Annie doesn't live here anymore." At her questioning look, he added. "She moved back to town about six months ago."

"Stupid," Casey muttered, and gripped her soggy veil more tightly. Shifting her gaze back to the fire, she said, more to herself than to him, "I should have known that she'd want to be back out on her own as quickly as possible."

She darted a quick look at him and he saw disappointment shadowing her eyes.

"How's she doing?"

"Pretty well." He lifted one shoulder in a half-hearted shrug. "You know Annie. Divorce is hard on anyone, but she'll be OK."

"I know she will."

"Yeah. I made it. She will, too."

"That's right." She straightened slightly and turned those green eyes on him. "Annie told me about your divorce. I'm sorry, Jake."

Discomfort rattled through him briefly as he looked into her eyes and saw sympathy and understanding. He shifted uneasily under her steady regard and wished she would change the subject. He didn't want to discuss Linda with her or anyone else. In fact, except for the valuable lesson Linda had taught him, he preferred to forget all about her.

"It was a long time ago," he said.

"Not so long. Only three years."

His gaze narrowed. Hell, he hadn't seen Casey in five years, but apparently his little sister kept the woman up to date on his life. "Is there anything Annie left out?"

"Not much," she admitted.

"Remind me to have a talk with my sister, huh?"

"How's Lisa?"

A small smile erased Jake's frown. Happened every time he thought about his three-year-old niece. It was simply impossible *not* to smile when thinking about the little terror.

"She's great. Driving Annie nuts."

For a too-brief moment Casey's smile joined his. "I haven't seen her in so long I probably wouldn't even recognize her." Her smile faded. "What about Lisa's father?"

He stiffened and unconsciously his hands curled into fists. As thoughts of Lisa could bring a smile, thoughts of her no-good father gave birth to sudden bursts of rage.

"Like you, he's been gone so long he wouldn't know his own daughter. Unlike you, he wouldn't care."

"That's a shame."

"Among other things."

Long silent minutes passed, and the only sounds

were the rain drumming on the tiled roof and the snap and hiss of the fire. Finally Casey broke the tension-filled quiet.

"I don't suppose you could give me a ride to town?"

"Can't."

"Why not?"

He frowned and shook his head. "Jeep's broken down and my foreman used the pickup to take his wife dancing. From the looks of this storm, they probably won't make it back until morning."

She stared at him as if she couldn't believe what he was saying. Well, he wasn't thrilled with the situation, either. She would just have to get used to it.

"Surely you have more than one Jeep and one truck on a ranch this size."

"Well, now," he drawled deliberately, "I surely do, ma'am. But I'm afraid my city car wouldn't fare any better than *your* car did in this mud."

"Oh."

"Yeah, oh."

"Can this day possibly get any worse?" she muttered.

"It's snowing," he offered.

A short strangled laugh shot from her throat. "Of course it is."

He watched her as she began to rub her hands briskly up and down her arms. As he stood there, a violent tremor rocked her. He felt like an idiot. While he was questioning her, she was no doubt catching pneumonia.

"You're never going to warm up while you're wearing that."

Her perfectly arched brows lifted high on her forehead. "Why, Jake," she said. "Are you trying to get me undressed?"

"Knock it off, Casey." He headed for the stove where he picked up the teakettle and carried it to the sink. As he filled it with water, he told her, "We've known each other too long for this. Just get out of the damned dress. You know where the bathroom is. I'll find you a robe or something."

When the kettle was half-full, he carried it to the stove, slammed it down on one of the burners, then turned on the fire underneath it. Then he stomped out of the kitchen without waiting to see if she was following his orders. The truth was, he admitted silently, he sure as hell didn't want to be anywhere near her when she started peeling off that dress. His little sister's friend or not, what she was doing to him was downright dangerous.

He marched down the long hallway to his bedroom at the back of the sprawling adobe-and-wood house. Throwing the door open, he absently noted the crash as the heavy oak panel hit the wall. But he was on a mission. Find something concealing for her to wear. Yes, he thought. Definitely concealing.

A burlap bag with a matching hood should do the trick.

Unfortunately he told himself as he stepped into the bathroom and glared at the garment hanging from the hook on the back of the door, all he had was a terry-cloth robe.

And a *short* robe at that.

Doesn't matter, he thought grimly. The important thing here was to get her dry. Then he'd dig out an old pair of sweats or something. Somehow, he had to survive the night, then get her the hell out of his life.

Again.

Clutching the robe in one fist, he marched back into his bedroom and came to a sudden stop at the foot of his bed.

In the past five years many things had changed. For one, he now slept in the master bedroom, not down the hall in the room where he'd grown up or even the guest house where he'd lived for a few years. He had changed most of the furnishings, painted the walls, installed new drapes. But the huge four-poster was the same. The same bed he'd slept in all his adult life.

And the same bed he'd found Casey in one night five long years ago.

Instantly the past was all around him, and he shuddered with the force of the memories.

There'd been a party in town. Casey's brothers had thrown themselves a farewell get-together. Since the Oakeses were leaving Simpson for the relatively big city of Morgan Hill, they'd decided to stage one last event for their friends.

He had left the party early, hoping to find some peace and quiet before his parents and sister returned to the ranch. He'd been living in the guest house then. A consideration, his father'd called it. A necessity was how Jake had thought of it. Even though working the family ranch was all he'd ever wanted to do, a thirty-year-old man needed more privacy than living in his parents' house could afford.

He'd walked through the dark guest house, not even bothering to turn on a lamp. In his mind, he could still hear the echo of his own footsteps in the empty rooms. He remembered feeling a little sorry for himself that the twins—and Casey—were moving away.

In his bedroom he'd plopped down onto the mattress to tug off his boots. He'd gotten one off and had just started on the other when her voice stopped him.

That so familiar voice had sounded different that night. Throaty, deep, filled with unspoken promises and just a quavering hint of nerves.

"I think you should know you are not alone."

Three

Jake had jumped to his feet, taken two quick steps to the bedside table and fumbled for the lamp switch.

Soft light dazzled the darkness, spilling over the woman waiting in his bed. Propped up with pillows behind her back, Casey lay beneath the covers. The sheet-topped quilt folded neatly across her breasts, she displayed just enough creamy flesh to let him know she was naked.

Jake drew one long unsteady breath, then deliberately took a step away from the bed. "What are you up to?"

She looked at him, then let her gaze slide to one side nervously. "Jake, I—"

"How did you get in here?"

"Annie gave me a key."

"Annie?" Damn, his little sister was in on this!

Was this setup some kind of a joke? But no. Instinctively he knew that whatever else she was up to, Cassandra Oakes wasn't kidding.

He flashed her another quick look and had to swallow back a groan. Her long blond hair lay across her shoulders and bare arms. Her green eyes shone with a passion he hadn't expected and didn't know quite how to handle.

Oh, he knew how he'd *like* to handle it. For months he'd been noticing his younger sister's friend—much to his disgust. God, he'd known Casey since she was ten! She was just a kid. At least he'd always thought of her as one. And yet lately, every time she showed up at the Parrish ranch, he was drawn to her. He'd found himself looking for her, hoping to see her.

And that worried him.

Hell, he was thirty years old. He was ready to settle down. He'd been to college. He'd had a chance to taste the rest of the world and had finally realized that the life he wanted was here. On the ranch.

But Casey Oakes was only nineteen—and barely out of high school.

What did she know about life? Or herself, for that matter? She didn't need *him* cluttering up her future just when it was beginning to open up in front of her.

So he had made up his mind to keep his desires in check. To keep a watchful distance from Casey until she'd had a chance to explore the world a bit.

But he'd never counted on having her ambush him in his bedroom.

"You'd better get out of here," he said past the hard knot of need lodged in his throat.

"But I've been waiting for you," she said. Jake watched as she held the covers to her and came up on her knees. She looked at him and shook her hair back away from her face.

He dragged a short harsh breath into straining lungs. Almost unwillingly his gaze shot to the swell of her breasts, where her armor of quilt and sheet was beginning to dip. Every breath she drew tantalized him, pushing him closer to the limits of his own endurance. His palms itched to cup her breasts. He could almost taste her sweet warmth.

Deliberately he clenched his hands at his sides and let his angry frustration color his voice.

"Well, now that I'm here," he said, "you can go."

"No."

"No?"

"Oh, Jake..." She leaned toward him, unknowingly letting that quilt drop another inch or two until the tops of her breasts were bared to his view. She held out one hand to him. "Don't you see? I've wanted this to happen for so long—and now we're moving away. I don't know when I'll be back."

That had occurred to him, as well. In fact, it was the main reason he'd left the party early. He hadn't felt like celebrating the fact that the one woman he was interested in was being spirited out of town. He wasn't a big believer in the old adage "Absence makes the heart grow fonder." No doubt, Casey would forget all about him in a year or two. As would he forget about her.

Which made it even more imperative that he got her the hell out of his bedroom.

"Casey, you shouldn't be here."

"This is exactly where I should be," she countered, and scooted to the edge of the bed, dragging the bedclothes with her. Climbing off the mattress, she walked to him and laid one hand on his forearm.

His skin seemed to burn at her touch, right through the fabric of his shirt. He clenched his jaw tight, determined to ignore the almost electric feel of her so close to him.

"I couldn't wait for you to take the first step anymore," she said softly, breathlessly. "I'm out of time. I *had* to tell you."

"Tell me what?" Say it, he pleaded silently. Say it and go.

"I love you."

Like a powerful fist to his midsection, Jake felt the blow. He stared into her eyes and saw everything he'd ever hoped to see shining back at him. Lord, how he wanted to tell her the same thing. He wanted to grab her, pull her tightly against him and lose himself in her. He wanted to slide into her warmth and hear her quiet moans of pleasure as they discovered each other. But he couldn't. It didn't matter if she claimed to be in love with him.

Nothing had changed. She was still too young. Too inexperienced to know what she wanted. She was still the kid who had followed him around the yard, peppering him with questions until he'd wanted to lock her in Annie's bedroom.

Despite the fact that she didn't look or feel like a kid at the moment, he couldn't take advantage of her feelings to ease the ache throbbing inside him. And he certainly couldn't expect a kid her age to make some kind of lifelong pledge of love.

Although he thought it might kill him, he forced himself to say, "Thank you, Casey. I appreciate it."

Her eyes mirrored the questions racing through her brain.

"You appreciate it?"

"Casey, I know you don't want to hear this—"

"Then don't say it. Please, Jake." Her fingers curled into the front of his shirt. "Don't say it."

"I have to." He reached up and covered her hand with one of his own. "I'm thirty years old, honey. You're just nineteen."

"I turn twenty next month."

"Twenty, then," he conceded. His thumb smoothed across her knuckles and he felt the warmth of that touch right to his bones. "You haven't even finished college yet."

"What does that have to do with us?"

"There is no 'us,'" he said, despite the pain that statement cost him.

"There could be."

He shook his head.

"Are you saying you don't feel anything for me?" she demanded.

"Casey…"

"I know you do, darn it. I know you feel *some-*

thing. I've seen the way you look at me. It's the same way I look at you."

Damn.

"Please, don't turn me away. I don't want to leave you." She stepped closer, reached up and cupped the back of his neck. Slowly she drew his head down to hers, then pressed her lips to his.

Jake groaned and forced himself to stand perfectly still under her gentle assault. The touch of her mouth was electrifying. Something sparked between the two of them. Something rare and magical. Still, he made no move to hold her, instead calling on the strength of his will to resist the incredible temptation she offered.

Then she dropped the quilt and sheet and reached up to wrap both arms around his neck. She pressed herself to him and he felt her hardened nipples rubbing against his chest. Desire rocketed through him, hard and hot. He wanted to do the right thing here, but Lord, he was only human.

When his arms closed around her bare back, a purr of satisfaction rumbled from her throat. His hands moved up and down the length of her spine, touching, exploring. Her lips parted and his tongue swept inside her mouth, tasting her for the first time. She was sweeter, more intoxicating than he had ever imagined. Instantly he knew that if he didn't stop that minute, he would never be able to let her go.

Abruptly he released her and took a step back.

"What's wrong?" she whispered. Her eyes were glazed with the smoldering fires of a passion just born. It was almost enough to make him forget his blasted attempt at nobility. Almost.

"What's wrong?" he repeated. "This." He bent down, scooped up the quilt and quickly draped it around her. "This whole thing is wrong," he snapped, then took another step away from her.

"How can it be when it feels so right?"

"Damn, Casey! I'm not made of stone, all right?" He glared at her briefly, then stomped past her to stare out the windows at the darkness outside. "Do us both a favor and leave, huh? Now. Before we both do something that can't be undone."

He heard her sniff and knew she was crying. Something cold settled in his chest, but he didn't look at her. He knew that if he turned and saw tears on her face, this hard-won battle would be lost. An eternity-filled moment later she spoke again.

"All right then, I'll leave."

Thank God.

"You're wrong, you know," she said, and he flinched at the pain in her voice. "About us. Age has nothing to do with love, Jake Parrish. And someday you're going to be sorry you sent me away tonight."

The memories ended abruptly as those last whispered words echoed in his mind.

He *had* been sorry.

Every night since.

But especially so tonight.

"So," she asked, "were you ever sorry?"

Jake turned slowly, inevitably, to face the woman standing in the open doorway of the bedroom. She'd finally gotten out of that wet wedding gown and was now draped in an oversize turquoise bath sheet.

"Sorrier than you'll ever know," he admitted finally.

"Good." Casey walked into the room holding his gaze with hers. Strange, the last time she'd been alone with this man she'd been stark naked. Now she wore only a towel. Judging by the flash of awareness in his eyes, he'd certainly noticed.

She'd only had to glance at him to know that he was reliving that long-ago night. Somehow it made her feel better to know that Jake, too, had regrets. She wondered what he would think if he knew her main regret was that she had allowed him to chase her away.

"Here." He held out his robe toward her. "You can wear this while I try to find you some sweats or something."

"Thanks," she said, and took the robe. She slipped into the garment, pulling it on right over the towel already covering her. Once the terry-cloth belt was tied at her waist, she turned back to him.

"I tossed my dress across the shower rod since it's still dripping mud. I hope that's OK."

"Sure."

He looked as uncomfortable as she felt.

History repeating itself?

"This isn't exactly how I imagined my wedding night turning out," she said suddenly on a laugh that held more nervousness than humor.

"What happened?" he asked. "Why are you here and not on some elaborate honeymoon?"

Another choked laugh shot from her throat before she could stop it. "I think the rules are you have to actually be *married* to go on a honeymoon."

His gaze narrowed and even in the semidarkness, she could see his familiar scowl.

Casey reached up and pushed her towel-dried but still-damp hair back from her face. Walking to the bed, Casey perched on the edge of the mattress, bracing her heels on the bed frame.

"What happened, Casey?" he asked again.

She set her elbows on her knees, glanced at Jake and shrugged. "Oh, nothing much. My groom decided at the last minute that marrying me wasn't such a good idea, after all." Her fingers plucked at the robe's worn fabric as she talked.

"He didn't show up?"

How much more humiliation was she supposed to survive in one day? It had been bad enough being jilted. Admitting the facts to Jake was another trip down embarrassment lane. But she supposed she might as well get used to the question. Lord knew she would probably be hearing it from everyone for the next several months.

"Yes," she finally said, "he was there. Long enough to give one of the ushers a note for me."

"A note?" Jake's voice was hard and disbelieving.

She held her breath when he walked to her side and sat down next to her. He made no move to touch her, though, and she didn't know whether she was relieved or disappointed.

"Yeah." She glanced at him and smiled halfheartedly. "It seems Steven suddenly had an urge to visit Mexico."

"Bastard."

"My thoughts exactly," she said, and unconsciously patted his hand. "At least at the time." But now that she thought about it, she was amazed to discover that the anger that had burst into life so swiftly had disappeared again almost as swiftly. Strange. All she felt now was relief—tinged with lingering traces of humiliation.

She hadn't been madly in love with Steven. Now she wasn't sure if she had even loved him at all. She had certainly liked him. Well, at least until today. He was a nice man, from what her mother liked to call a good family. Translation, Casey thought, *rich*.

Their parents had wanted the match and she and Steven had simply drifted into it. She couldn't even recall her ex-fiancé actually proposing. It had simply been taken for granted.

She scowled, lifted one hand and rubbed at her forehead. The mother of all headaches was just beginning to throb.

"I'm sorry, Casey."

"Why?" she asked. "You weren't the one rejecting me this time."

"Let's not go there, all right?"

"Why not?" She turned her head and looked directly into his eyes. The eyes she used to dream about. "This *is* my wedding night, after all. What better thing to at least *talk* about than sex? Or the lack thereof."

"I left the kettle on," he said, and moved to get up. "Why don't we go and get you some hot tea?"

"I turned it off when the water boiled," she told him, and waved him back down to the mattress.

"Casey," he said, and shifted a bit farther from her, "you've had a bad day. Why not just get some sleep, huh?"

"I don't want to sleep, Jake." In fact, she'd never been more awake. Ordinarily she wouldn't have considered seeking him out and asking him about that night—but now that the fates had provided her with the opportunity, she really wanted to know just why he'd turned her away.

He stood up abruptly and began to pace.

"Oh, relax," she told him. "I'm not going to attempt another seduction. You convinced me a long time ago that you weren't interested. I won't ask you twice."

"Huh!" He snorted a laugh and quickened his aimless pacing. "Not interested? I don't remember saying that."

Casey blinked. Swiveling her head, she followed his progress around the room while trying to ignore the sudden flare of heat in the pit of her stomach.

Quickly her brain raced back over the memory of that night. She recalled the feel of his hands on her bare flesh. The taste of his mouth on hers. His strangled breath. But mostly she remembered the gentle yet firm way he'd turned her away.

"Do you mean that you *did* want me?" she asked, her voice hesitant.

"*Want* you?" He laughed shortly. "Oh, I guess you could say that. I could hardly walk for a week."

Casey blinked again. She sat up straighter and half turned to look at him. Standing beside the window, he held the drapes back with one hand and stared out into the night. Flashes of white drifted past the window.

"It's still snowing," she said softly, her gaze locked on his tight features.

"Yeah. Not heavily, though."

"If you wanted me, why did you turn me down?" She had to be crazy. Or at least masochistic. Wasn't being jilted at the altar enough for one day? Did she really *have* to know the answer to that question? Even if it meant adding more humiliation to an already full day?

Yes. She did.

Besides, Jake's rejection was five long years ago. All she wanted now was the reason for it.

When he didn't answer, she repeated. "Why, Jake?"

He glanced at her, his expression stony.

"I had to. You were just a kid." He shifted his gaze back to the snow. "A man just doesn't take advantage of a kid's...crush."

"A crush?" She shook her head at him, but he didn't see her. "I *loved* you."

"You were too young to know anything about love."

"According to who?"

"Me."

"So you decided to be noble."

"I *decided* to do the right thing," he corrected as his fingers tightened on the drapery fabric. "But yeah. I wanted you."

A knot of regret for chances missed lodged in her throat. Her gaze swept over him and she noted that he hadn't changed much in the past five years. Oh, she knew he'd been married. Just as she knew his marriage had been a painful one. Annie had kept Casey up-to-date on him over the years.

But Jake's wanting her?

That was something she was willing to bet that Annie had never known.

God, how she wished *she* had known.

She heard herself ask the next inevitable question. "When did you stop wanting me?"

Jake turned his head and gave her a tight smile. "I'll let you know as soon as it happens."

"You mean...?"

He inhaled sharply, turned away from the window and started for the doorway. "We shouldn't be talking about this," he muttered thickly.

Stunned, Casey scooted off the bed and intercepted him before he could leave the room. Her hand on his arm, she looked up at him, willing him to meet her gaze. At last, clearly reluctantly, he did.

The expression on his face, in his eyes, rocketed through her. Desire. Want. Need. All the old feelings that had burned so brightly between them so long ago were still there. Buried and carefully ignored for far too long, they were alive again now, and there was no way to stop them. Even if she'd wanted to.

Casey swallowed heavily. If anything, those emotions, those feelings, seemed suddenly stronger than ever before. Maybe that long-ago night and even her botched wedding were just foils used by fate to bring them together when the time was finally right.

For one incredible moment she felt as though she'd been given a second chance.

"Jake," she said softly, "I'm all grown-up now."

His gaze swept over her. "I noticed."

She smiled. A skittering of warmth shot from her fingertips, still resting on his forearm, straight to her heart. "I told you I wouldn't ask you again..."

"A wise decision."

"...but I didn't say what my answer would be if *you* asked *me*."

"Casey..."

"I would say...*yes*."

The world stopped.

She knew it had, because her heart wasn't beating and she was still alive. It was as if everything inside her and around her was waiting for Jake's reaction.

Slowly he lifted one hand to cup her cheek. His thumb traced over her cheekbone with tender reverence. She turned her face into his touch and heard his breath catch.

"You're crazy," he whispered.

"Maybe. But I don't think so."

He shook his head. "This isn't about me, Casey. You're just reacting to being stood up. And that's no reason to do this."

"You're wrong, Jake." She turned her face into his palm and left a kiss on his callused flesh. "This has nothing to do with anyone outside this room."

He sucked in a deep breath.

"That night has always been with me," she said softly. "For whatever reason we have a second chance. Tonight." She lifted one hand and covered his fingers, still cupping her cheek. "Maybe you made the right decision five years ago," she conceded. "But whether you did or not, that time is over. Done. For both our sakes make the right decision tonight, too."

Another long moment passed in silence.

"Right or wrong," he whispered as his gaze caressed her face. "This time I'm asking, Casey. Stay with me tonight."

"Yes," she said on a sigh, and rose on her toes to meet his kiss.

Four

Emotion flickered across his features. She thought for one awful moment that he was going to change his mind.

Then his mouth came down on hers in a hard fierce rush of need. There was nothing hesitant or reluctant in his touch. Instead, she felt his hunger as sharply as she did her own. She gasped at the strength of the desire pulsing through her. Five years disappeared as if they'd never been, and once again, Casey was that twenty-year-old girl offering the man she loved everything she had to give.

Only this time he gave back more than she could have hoped.

He parted her lips with his tongue and invaded her warmth with a deep thrust that promised greater delight to come. A shower of sparks ignited inside her at the intimate caress, and she leaned into him, wanting more. He groaned under his breath and reached for the belt of her robe. In one smooth motion he untied the knot and slid the maroon terry cloth down off her shoulders to puddle on the floor.

Casey shivered as his fingers slipped beneath the edge of the bath sheet still wrapped around her. In less than a heartbeat the towel, too, lay on the braided rug at her feet.

Her long still-damp hair hung down her back and she trembled slightly. But then he pulled her tightly to him and his hands began to make swift eager strokes up and down her spine, and her shivering had nothing to do with the chill in the room.

Everything within her responded magically to his touch. It was as if he had reached into her soul and turned a light on all the dark lonely places she had tried for so long to hide. She arched into him, wanting more, needing more.

He groaned and broke their kiss, lifting his head to gasp for air like a dying man. For one long heart-stopping moment he looked at her. She felt his gaze sweep over her nude body like a caress, and any embarrassment she might have felt disappeared under the light of passion glimmering in his eyes.

Suddenly, though, he took a half step back from her, and through gritted teeth asked, "Casey, are you sure about this?"

If she hadn't been sure before, she would have been the moment he touched her. This was right. She knew it. She felt it.

It was five long years since she'd been with him

in his bedroom. She had done plenty of growing up in that time, and if he wanted to get rid of her again, it wouldn't be as easy for him now.

"I'm standing here in your bedroom stark naked, and you can ask me that?"

He rubbed the back of his neck as his gaze moved over her again. Thoroughly. "I have to ask. I have to know. I have to know that *you* know what you're doing. This is your last chance, Casey." His jaw tightened and he sucked in a sharp short breath. "If you want to change your mind, say so now."

There it was. His halfhearted attempt to get her to leave. A part of her told her she should take it and run. A voice in the back of her mind shouted for caution. Reason. Logic. But what she was feeling had nothing to do with logic. She took a step closer to him.

"I want you to make love to me, Jake."

He groaned.

"I *need* you to make love to me, Jake." She reached out one hand to touch his chest. He flinched as if burned. "Now."

He yanked his shirttail free of his jeans, then tore the shirt off, sending buttons flying into the shadowed corners of the room.

Her mouth dry, Casey watched as he hurriedly pulled the rest of his clothes off. When he finally stood in front of her completely naked, she sucked in a breath and stared helplessly.

Years of hard work on the ranch had toned his body into a mass of sculpted muscle. His broad chest was tanned, with just a sprinkling of dark hair dusting his sun-bronzed skin. His shoulders looked powerful, his arms strong. Her gaze shifted to follow the narrow trail of dark hair that swept down his abdomen.

She gasped at first sight of his sex. Hard and ready, he looked huge, and just for a moment, doubt leaped into Casey's mind. Then he reached for her and all thought danced out the window to disappear in the softly falling snow.

Cradled close against him, she reveled in the feel of her hard nipples pressed to his chest. She loved the sensation of skin on skin. Warmth to warmth. Hard to soft.

His arousal poked at her belly, and a slow curl of heat began to unfold between her legs. She moved against him and a low growl of pleasure rumbled from his throat. He dipped his head to hers and once more plundered her mouth. Casey wrapped her arms around his neck to steady herself, then returned his touch with her own. Her tongue stroked his, and a well of satisfaction burst open inside her as his arms tightened around her in response.

As she gave herself over to the delights spiraling within her, Jake slipped one of his hands from her back to smooth over her hip, then slide between their bodies. Her breath caught as his fingertips moved through the nest of blond curls at the apex of her thighs.

Confidently he continued his exploration and smiled against her mouth as she parted her legs for him. As his fingers dipped lower, his other hand cupped her behind and held her steady.

She jumped slightly when he located a single spot of sensation. He groaned and deepened his kiss, silently demanding her attention, her passion. As his tongue thrust in and out of her mouth, his fingers moved over her most intimate flesh.

She trembled violently when a spear of delight lanced through her. Breaking his kiss, she let her head fall back and concentrated solely on the magic in his touch. Her eyes slid shut and bright colors swarmed through the room. Her knees wobbled and she tried desperately to lock them into place. If she moved, he might stop and she knew she didn't want *that.*

As if sensing her unsteadiness, Jake lifted her easily, and carried her the few steps to the bed. Throwing the bedspread to the foot of the mattress with one hand, he eased her down.

Cool clean sheets caressed her back, but before she could enjoy the decadent sensation of lying naked in bed, Jake was there. Everywhere.

As if finally unleashing his passion, he devoured her with his mouth and hands. His lips came down on one of her hardened nipples, and Casey gasped at the almost unbearable pleasure shooting through her. Before she could become accustomed to his mouth at her breast, he dragged his teeth lightly across the sensitive flesh.

"Jake!" She half lifted herself off the mattress, trying to follow him as he shifted position. "Don't stop. Please, don't stop."

"We're just getting started," he said, and gently pushed her back down onto the bed. Dipping his head, he took first one nipple, then the other into his mouth. Using his lips and tongue and teeth, he drove her higher and higher into a world she'd never known existed before.

Casey moved and twisted in his arms, enjoying his attentions, yet craving something she knew lay just out of reach.

She had never known. Never guessed that it could be like this. Jake touched her, and her body turned to fire. Her mind dissolved and coherent thought was impossible. Heat shimmered on her skin, soaking through to her bones and lighting up her soul in a wild inferno of sensation.

The calluses on his gentle hands scratched her smooth flesh, reminding her of his strength. Whisker stubble scraped her breasts, lending another sensation to his lavish kisses.

It was as if he wanted to know every part of her. Feel all of her. Kiss and taste her. His strong fingers explored her body as he suckled and tenderly pulled at her nipples.

Then he lifted his head and she looked up, meeting his gaze boldly.

Desire etched plainly into his chiseled features, he stared down at her with eyes darkened with a passion that only grew stronger as the moments flew past.

She looked wild, abandoned. Her eyes glittered with desire and her lips pouted as if begging to be kissed.

Jake surrendered gladly, taking her mouth with his as if his life depended on it. And at the moment, he admitted, it probably did. He tasted her sweetness and loved her eager response.

He'd been right to turn her down so long ago.

The wait had definitely been worth it.

Her tongue swept over his and he groaned, relishing the electricity that shimmered between them. He had never felt so alive. His body hummed with restless energy and demands he hadn't experienced in far too long. He needed to be inside her. Needed it more than he cared to acknowledge.

Breaking their kiss, he moved to kneel between her legs. Drawing her knees up on either side of him, he looked down at her open pink flesh and rubbed his thumb slowly, deliberately, over the hard nub of her pleasure.

Her body twisted, her back arched and her head tipped back into the mound of pillows behind her. Two fingers slipped into her damp tight heat and she inhaled sharply as if caught unawares. As he continued to stroke her, she planted her feet and lifted herself into his touch. His fingers moved deftly on the most sensitive part of her flesh, and her hips pumped in a wild rocking motion that pushed him nearer the edge of control.

"Help me, Jake," she whispered brokenly. Her fingers curled into the sheet beneath her. "That feels so good," she managed to say on a gasp. "I need…"

"I know, baby," he said, his voice low and strangled. "I need it, too." Jake swallowed heavily, winced against the pain of his aching groin and moved his hands to cup her behind. He couldn't wait another moment to claim her. To slide into her heat and become a part of her. He had never known such want. Such a desperate longing to join with a woman. To feel her body close around his. To taste her. To swallow her breath and make it his own.

Lifting her hips for his entry, he pushed himself deeply into the warmth he had waited so long to find.

She gasped in pain.

He froze.

Her back bowed.

He cursed.

Her eyes flew open.

Staring into those meadow green eyes, he managed to snarl. "Why didn't you tell me you were a virgin?"

She wiggled her hips, inhaled sharply, then sighed as she wrapped her arms around his neck. "Does it make a difference?"

Deep within her tight hot body, he throbbed for release. The damage was done. There was no going back. Even if he wanted to. Which he didn't.

"Not anymore," he said, and eased his body out of hers only to push his way inside again.

"Jake!"

Her nails dug into his shoulders. Her legs lifted and locked around his hips. He moved and she moved with him. He became caught up in the age-old rhythm, and everything but the need for completion disappeared from his mind.

Sliding one hand between their bodies, Jake found again the tender nub of flesh that held the key to her release. As he stroked her, he watched wonder slowly dawn on her face. Her eyes closed, she bit down hard on her bottom lip and lifted her hips high, arching into his touch, straining.

When the first tremors hit her, she shouted his name and dug her fingernails even deeper into his back. The ripples of satisfaction coursing through her grabbed at him. Her body convulsed and tightened around his, squeezing him until with one final thrust, he emptied himself into her and collapsed like a dead man atop her.

He tried to speak. But first he had to find out if he could still breathe.

A tentative shallow breath of air entered his lungs and he accepted it gratefully. His heart felt as though it was about to burst through the wall of his chest. He knew he should move. He was probably crushing her slender body, but somehow, he couldn't find the strength or the will to lift himself off her.

He'd never experienced anything like that before. Oh, making love had always been good. Although he hadn't been with a woman in longer than he cared to think about. Ever since Linda, Jake had steered clear of females. Once burned, forever shy.

Still, had it been so long that he'd forgotten how explosive it could be? How incredible?

No. He frowned and finally rolled to one side of her. It wasn't just making love. It was making love with Casey that had made the experience so... He let *that* thought fade away. It was much safer to attack than to sit idly by.

"Why didn't you tell me?"

"Hmm?"

Jake watched her as she stretched and *smiled,* for God's sake.

"I said, why the hell are you still a virgin?"

"I'm not anymore," she replied in a well-satisfied tone. "Thank you very much."

"Thank you?"

"Well, yeah." She shot him a quick confused look. "Sorry, I've never done this before. What is one supposed to say after one has been thoroughly..."

"Ravished?" he finished, scowling at her. "Deflowered?"

She laughed. "Deflowered? Jeez, Jake, you sound like a Puritan!"

Puritan? Him?

"Don't worry, OK? I don't think my father even *owns* a shotgun."

"Casey, you could have told me."

"You didn't ask."

"I didn't think I had to. You had a fiancé. You were getting married today."

"You didn't notice that the dress was white?"

"I didn't think that meant anything anymore."

"Now you know."

He shoved one hand through his hair and stared up at the ceiling. Shadows darted across the open wood beams.

"You should have told me."

"If I had, you might not have wanted to—"

"Damn right," he interrupted.

"See?" She stretched and winced a bit at the movement.

He closed his eyes briefly. Damn. Her first time and he'd treated her like she'd done the deed a hundred times before.

"Did I hurt you?" he asked, already dreading the answer.

"*Hurt* me?" She pushed herself up on one elbow and looked down at him. "It was...wonderful. I didn't know it would be like that at all."

"What were you expecting?"

"Oh, I don't know." She sighed and drew one finger down the middle of his chest. "I suppose I knew it would feel nice, but how could I have expected *anything* as dramatic as that?"

He grabbed her hand and held it tight. Hard to believe, but one simple touch of her finger had his body leaping to life again.

Looking up at her, he studied her fine almost elegant features, the mass of blond hair ruffled around her head like some sort of rumpled halo and the soft shine in her eyes. What in hell was wrong with her fiancé? Why hadn't he married her? And for God's sake, why hadn't he *slept* with her?

Before he could stop himself, he blurted out that last question.

Immediately her features shifted, hardened. She pulled her hand free of his, then flopped over onto her back and crossed her arms over her naked breasts.

"It never came up." Then she stopped shortly, thought about what she'd said and added, "No pun intended."

"I don't get it," he admitted, and levered himself

up on one elbow to look down at her. "I didn't think anybody waited for marriage anymore."

"Excuse me for being a dinosaur."

"That's not what I meant."

"If you're thinking I saved myself for *you,* forget it."

"I didn't say that, either." Had talking to Casey *always* been this confusing?

"I came to you once and you made yourself very clear. You weren't interested."

"I think," he said wryly, "that we've pretty much disposed of that notion."

Her lips twitched. "You have a point."

"What'd you say his name was?"

She paused for a moment as if trying to remember what they'd been talking about. Then offhandedly she said, "Steven."

"Steven," he repeated quietly. "The man must be out of his mind."

She drew her head back and turned to grin at him. "Why, Jake Parrish! I believe that is the *nicest* thing you've ever said to me."

His eyes rolled heavenward as he turned onto his back to stare at the ceiling again. "Let's return to what just happened."

"Yes," she agreed, moving to rest her head on his shoulder. "Let's."

"Cut it out, Casey," he warned, and tried to inch farther away from her.

"You can't pretend you don't want me anymore, Jake," she said, and skimmed one hand down his body toward his already hard arousal.

"Casey, dammit!" He caught up her hand and held it tightly. "You're a *virgin*. My sister's friend. A...a *kid!*"

"Taking your objections one at a time," she said, pausing only to plant a quick kiss on his chest, "as you have no doubt observed, I am not a virgin anymore."

"Lord."

"As to being Annie's friend, of course I am. So what? Everybody is *somebody's* friend."

"Knock it off, Casey," he grumbled as her teeth scraped across his flat nipple, sending shock waves of desire through him.

She lifted her head and smiled at him. "As for the last objection, I think even you have to agree that I'm not exactly a kid anymore, either."

He inhaled sharply, then released the breath slowly, painfully.

Casey smiled to herself. He was weakening. She glanced below his waist. Well, not *all* of him was weakening. Hesitantly she moved to touch him.

He gasped through clenched teeth, and as her fingers curled around him, she felt him shudder. An incredible feeling of power rose in her. Jake Parrish wanted her. He could deny it all he wanted to. His body couldn't hide from her.

Her heart felt full enough to pop. Now she knew why she'd been so relieved when Steven jilted her. Of course she hadn't wanted to marry the man her parents had chosen for her.

She still had too many deep feelings for Jake.

"A *virgin*," he muttered thickly, disgustedly.

Casey leaned over him, her hair falling over one shoulder to drag gently across his chest. She placed a brief tantalizing kiss on his lips, then lifted her head to look at him.

"Jake, one virgin more or less isn't going to mean the downfall of the nation. You're not a criminal. You didn't tie me down and force me."

At that notion he groaned again.

She grinned. "If anything, *I* took advantage of *you*."

"What?"

"Sure," she said, warming to her subject. "I seduced you with my wicked city wiles and then had my way with you. You being a poor innocent country boy, you had no choice but to go along."

A reluctant half smile hovered around his mouth. "Feel better?"

"Maybe," he said.

"Well," she whispered as she bent to kiss his flat nipple, "I have an idea on just how you might *positively* feel better."

"Casey," he said, and cupped her face with one callused hand, "we can't do this again. Once was a mistake. Twice would be downright foolish."

She winced inwardly, but gave him a smile, anyway. "Be a fool with me then, Jake." She leaned over him, dropping soft tender kisses on his brow, his eyes, his cheeks. "Just for tonight be a fool with me."

Five

She held her breath, waiting.

Her stomach fluttered nervously. Her mouth was dry and she was sure that if she held her hands out, she would see them tremble.

Ridiculous. She'd just made love with the man. What was left to be anxious about? But she knew the answer to that question. Their brief passionate encounter had been exactly what her mother used to warn her about. When hormones and desire get out of control, sometimes you do things you wouldn't ordinarily do.

If they made love again, though, it would be because she and Jake both wanted to experience it all again without the wild mind-blurring haze of maddening desire to cloud the issue.

His brow furrowed slightly, then his blue eyes narrowed as he looked up at her.

"What?" she asked.

"Something just occurred to me." He pushed himself up onto both elbows and tipped his head to one side. "You were a virgin and didn't tell me."

"I thought we'd covered that."

"What else didn't you tell me?"

"What do you mean?" What else *was* there?

"Casey, are you...do you...? Hell. Are you on any kind of birth control?"

Oh, Lord. She felt her jaw drop.

"Damn." Jake dropped back onto the bed like he'd been shot.

"I didn't think," she said quickly. "I've always wanted children and Steven said it was up to me." She frowned thoughtfully. Steven hadn't even cared enough to express an opinion about whether or not to have children. She'd never considered preventing a child. For as long as she could remember, she'd wanted a family of her own.

She touched her flat belly and wondered if Jake had just given her the child she'd longed for.

He saw her movement and obviously misinterpreted her expression. "There's probably nothing to worry about," he said. "The chances that you actually conceived on your first time must be pretty slim." He inhaled sharply. "But if you did, we'll think of something."

She lay down next to him again and rested her head on his chest. Beneath her ear, his heartbeat thudded steadily. It was a long moment before he draped his arm around her. When he did, Casey smiled.

"I'm sorry, Casey," he said softly. "It never should have happened. I can't even remember the last time I acted before thinking it through."

"Don't be sorry." She tipped her head back to look at him. "I've wanted this to happen for a long time."

He gave a choked laugh and shook his head. "You don't make it easy for a man to feel guilty."

"There's nothing to be guilty about."

"You might be pregnant," he reminded her, and his hand on her arm tightened briefly.

"But probably not," she said. "You said yourself the chances were slim." Although, she added silently, if it was going to happen to anyone, it would probably happen to her. She had always been *lucky* that way.

"Yeah. Look." He gave her a quick pat, then moved away and eased off the mattress. Standing beside the bed, he said, "We'd better find you some dry clothes. You can stay in Annie's old room tonight. I'll call a tow for your car in the morning."

"Jake—"

"Casey, it's over."

"It doesn't have to be," she said in a rush. She didn't want this time with him to be finished so quickly. For whatever reason, she'd been granted this one night with the man she'd dreamed about for years. And just this once, she was going to do what she felt she *needed* to do. Something for her. Something to hold on to in the nights to come. Something to remember forever.

She wanted this one night with Jake more than she'd ever wanted anything. And this time, she was willing to fight to have it.

"Casey, we can't take another chance."

"Isn't there another way? Something we can do?"

He stared down at her, and in the half-light, she saw the indecision on his features. Steeling herself with a deep breath, she sat up straighter and let the sheet drop from in front of her. His gaze shifted to her breasts, and she watched as lines of strain deepened in his face.

She leaned toward him, extending one hand. "Jake, this is our night. The night we were always meant to have."

"You don't really believe that, do you?"

"Yes. I do." Her fingers trembled and her arm began to ache, but still, she held her hand out toward him. "For some unknown reason, we were brought together tonight. We would be crazy to turn away from it."

"Dammit, Casey..."

A strong gust of wind rattled the windowpane. She gave him a small smile. "It's a sign."

"It's a storm." One corner of his mouth lifted slightly as his gaze moved over her again.

"Just tonight, Jake."

"I must be out of my mind," he muttered as he knelt on the mattress and gathered her close.

Casey's pent-up breath escaped in a slow sigh, and she melted against him. The warmth of him surrounded her, and she told herself to remember it all. Her breasts flattened against his broad chest. His arms wrapped tightly around her, his breath on her hair, her name sliding from his throat on a whisper.

His lips met hers in a slow languorous kiss as he eased them both down onto the mattress. He tasted her bottom lip, then the top. His teeth nibbled at her mouth, teasing her with a promise of more to come. Casey lay across his chest, a willing captive. He cradled the back of her head, threading his fingers through her hair.

She'd never known that the scalp could be an erogenous zone. But the feel of his fingers against her head sent needles of awareness pricking along her spine.

In one easy motion he rolled over, tucking her beneath him. He didn't break their kiss. Instead, he deepened it, his tongue caressing, tasting her. She welcomed his gentle invasion and released the last bit of anxiety hiding in one corner of her heart.

She ran her hands across his back, measuring the corded muscles beneath her palms. So strong yet so gentle. His body hovered over hers, covering her, protecting her, enticing her with its very presence. Arching into him, she silently demanded more. She wanted to feel his hands and his mouth on her breasts again.

She wanted to feel it all.

Jake shifted slightly and trailed a line of damp slow kisses along the line of her slender throat. He smoothed his left hand over her body, skimming across her flesh with the leisurely tender touch he should have given her before. Her first time should have been special. Gentle. He couldn't change what had already happened. But he could give her this. Give them both this.

He bent his head to take one of her nipples into his mouth. She gasped with pleasure, which sent identical waves of delight rippling through him—and he didn't dare ask himself why.

Sliding his left hand across her belly, he cupped her center, letting her damp heat touch him, warm him. Something in his chest tightened, threatening to choke off his air. He dipped one finger inside her and groaned at the feel of her body surrounding him. She instinctively drew him deeper within.

As a second finger moved to join the first, he switched his attentions to her other breast, clamping his lips around the hard pink nub and drawing at it gently. She groaned and spiked her fingers through his hair, holding his head to her breast as if afraid he would stop.

His heart pounded furiously and he wanted to tell her that he had no intention of stopping, but he couldn't bring himself to abandon her breasts even that long.

Brushing his thumb gently across the small hard button of her sex, he felt her body jump in response. His heartbeat accelerated, and the throbbing ache in his groin almost drove him to the point of madness. He had never known such need. Such want. Her slender curvy body beneath his hands brought him more delight than he had ever found before, and he wanted to know all of her. Reluctantly he lifted his head long enough to claim her lips with his.

He swallowed her sigh as his tongue darted in and out of her mouth. She met him stroke for stroke. Caress for caress. Her untutored enthusiasm fed the fire raging within him until he thought he might explode.

When neither of them could wait another moment to be joined, Jake reached across her to the bedside table. Yanking open the drawer, he grabbed a small foil packet and slammed the drawer shut again. Hurriedly he provided the protection he should have offered her before. Then he positioned himself between her legs and slowly pushed his way into her warmth. He watched as passion took her. Her head tipped back into the pillows and her eyes slid shut.

"Jake..." she groaned softly, and held her arms out for him.

He had to fight his instinct to move into her embrace. Keeping perfectly still in an effort to control his own overpowering need, he inhaled deeply, reminding himself that this time was for her. Buried deep within her body, he looked down at their joining and gently brushed her most sensitive spot with his fingertips.

She swiveled her hips, and the movement made beads of sweat break out on his forehead. He bit down on the inside of his cheek and concentrated solely on pleasuring her.

Casey threw both hands behind her head and clutched desperately at the feather pillows. She needed something stable to hold on to as her world began to splinter around her. His fingers didn't stop.

Didn't slow. Over and over, he rubbed and stroked her center until she felt a helpless wail building in her chest.

She rocked her hips in a frenzied attempt to scale the peak she'd just begun climbing. And every movement drove Jake's hardness deeper within her, tormenting her from the inside.

Her breath coming in short rapid gasps, she opened her eyes and looked at him. His gaze was locked on hers. She couldn't look away. Green eyes stared into blue. A muscle in his jaw twitched, and she realized that the same agony of need piercing her touched him, too.

"Jake," she whispered, and reached one hand out to him.

He grabbed it as though it was a lifeline in a stormy sea. Their fingers laced together, she held on tightly as the first shock wave of delight hit her.

Starting off slowly, it built and built, the pleasure deepening, blossoming until the last soul-shattering spasm shook through her. She heard someone scream, and a small corner of her mind recognized the voice as her own.

Still holding her hand, Jake covered her body with his and rocked his hips against her. Small ripples of sensation continued to throb inside her. His steady thrusts heightened the sensation. She locked her legs around his hips, pulling him deeper, closer. Before she knew it or could prepare for it, another wave of tiny explosions battered her. Casey cried out and felt his breath fan her cheek. She squeezed his hand tightly when he stiffened, groaned and surrendered himself to her.

She shifted, draped one leg over his and snuggled her head more firmly into the curve of his shoulder. Jake scowled into the darkness and tugged the sheet higher up over her. Then, keeping one arm draped around the sleeping woman, he stared into the darkness.

What in hell had he been thinking?

Disgusted, he admitted that he hadn't been thinking at all. He'd reacted. Like a damn high-school kid who couldn't get a grip on his rampaging hormones, he'd grabbed at what was offered without a thought for the consequences.

She muttered something in her sleep, chuckled softly, then wriggled even closer.

Small electrical charges fluttered through him and he frowned. All right, so it was more than hormones. He had never experienced anything like that in his life. Just touching her set off some sort of chain-reaction firework display. There was more at work here than simple desire.

But he wasn't about to go *there*.

He had done the love-and-marriage thing once. It hadn't worked. No way was he going to try it again.

Still, he admitted silently, there was another problem to consider. He'd taken her virginity, for God's sake. Something he'd always managed to avoid before. Dammit, he hadn't been raised to sleep with a virgin and casually walk away.

Especially when that virgin was Casey Oakes.

Not to mention the fact that there was a chance, however slim, that she could be pregnant.

What was he supposed to do now?

Shaking his head, he shifted his gaze to the windows on his left and tried to clear his mind. Just for the moment. He'd be able to think more clearly if he got at least a couple of hours' sleep.

Stars winked at him from a clear sky. The storm had finally cleared out. Maybe that was a good sign.

"Omigosh, omigosh." Annie snatched the muddy wet wedding dress down from the shower rod and raced with it into the kitchen.

"Mommy," the little girl left behind called out, "I still hafta go potty."

But Annie was on a mission and didn't hear her daughter's complaint. Rushing into the kitchen where her father, aunt and uncle sat around the table waiting for Jake to wake up, she demanded, "Look! Look what I found!"

"For heaven's sake," Aunt Emma said with a sniff. "What on earth happened to that beautiful dress?"

"Where'd you get it?" Frank Parrish asked his daughter.

"In the bathroom," Annie told him. "Hanging over the shower rod."

"Should have left it there," Emma said, lifting one black eyebrow at the trail of mud across the Spanish tiles.

"Wonder why Jake has a wedding dress?" Uncle Harry scratched his chin thoughtfully.

"Don't you see?" Annie dropped the dress into her father's lap and looked at each of her thick-headed relatives one at a time. "*This* is what Jake meant on the phone last night."

"This what?"

She flashed a quick dumbfounded look at Harry and went on, concentrating on her father. "Jake said he'd finally succeeded in getting something he'd wanted for a long time."

"Yeah?"

"This must be it!" Annie brushed a stray lock of hair back out of her eyes and grinned at her dad. "Jake got *married!*"

Aunt Emma's dark brown eyes looked like saucers with spilled coffee in the center.

"Married?" Uncle Harry repeated. "Who got married?"

"Jake."

"Annie," her father warned, "you don't know that for sure."

"Why else would he have a wedding dress here?" She shook her head until another long strand of black hair fell out of the neat bun and lay across her shoulder. "What a rat! Keeping this a secret from us. Why wasn't I invited?"

Frank Parrish ran one gnarled hand over the mud-spattered lace gown. "If he *is* married, how did *this* happen? He tied her to his saddle and dragged her through the mud until she said, 'I do'?"

"Oh, I don't know." Annie turned away and started pacing, a soft smile on her face. "It doesn't matter how it happened. I just want to know who."

"Mommy!"

The shout came from down the hall.

"Lisa!" Annie gasped, shamefaced, and started for the door. "I forgot all about her—and she has to go potty."

Aunt Emma sniffed again. "Potty! *Really*. The child's probably had an accident by now."

"Potty is a perfectly fine word." Annie shot her aunt an annoyed look and not for the first time wondered what her sweet befuddled uncle Harry had ever seen in the sharp-tongued old biddy.

"A child should not be taught to shout in public about bodily functions."

"She's not *in* public. She's—" Annie stopped short. She didn't owe anyone an explanation about how she raised her daughter. Least of all Emma. "Never mind," she said, and hastened her steps.

"Mommy!" Lisa's voice was louder, more demanding. "Who's da lady in da bed?"

Emma gasped.

"What?" Harry asked. "What lady? Where?"

"Uh-oh," Frank muttered, and pushed himself out of his chair. Following his daughter, he headed into the hall toward his son's room.

Emma and Harry were right behind him.

Jake's bedroom door was wide open. A slash of morning sunlight lay across the big four-poster and the two people under the sheets.

Annie skidded to a sudden stop at the threshold and her father crashed into her, pushing her the rest of the way into the room. Behind them, Aunt Emma gasped again. Annie glanced at her. She clutched a church newsletter in her beringed chubby hands and was frantically waving it back and forth in front of her flushed face.

Harry pushed his round wire spectacles higher on his nose and peered over his wife's formidable shoulder.

Lisa, a black-haired, blue-eyed, twenty-five-pound bundle of energy, stood at the foot of the bed, holding her crotch and jumping from foot to foot.

"Morning, son," Frank offered.

"Dad." Jake sat up slowly and looked at the small crowd. "Annie."

"Unco Jake," Lisa demanded again, "Who's da naked lady?"

Just then the naked lady sat up beside Jake, clutching the sheet to her chest like a warrior's shield. She blinked wildly, looked at the people in the doorway, then smiled sheepishly.

"The lady," Annie told her daughter, "is your aunt Casey."

"Can *she* take me to go potty?"

Six

Jake tossed a look over his shoulder at the snow-dusted house behind him. Inside his sister was closeted with Casey, and Lord only knew what *she* was saying. He frowned thoughtfully and hoped that his uncle Harry had been able to keep his aunt Emma from grabbing the phone.

From the moment he and Casey had been discovered together, he'd seen Emma's dialing finger twitching. She could hardly wait to get busy spreading the latest gossip. News of finding Jake and a new bride in bed was good. News of finding Jake and someone else's bride in bed was even better!

Wryly he remembered that when he'd decided to divorce Linda, Jake hadn't had to tell a soul. Emma had taken care of notifying the town. And had managed it all in just under two hours.

"Well, son..." his father said softly. Jake turned his head to look at him. "What are you going to do about this?"

"What is there *to* do?" Defensive. Why did he sound so defensive? He was an adult. So was Casey. It was no one else's business if two consenting adults spent the night together. He scowled and hunched his sheepskin-clad shoulders. If that was true, why did he feel like a teenager caught on the couch with his hand up a girl's skirt?

"Jake," the older man tried again, "I saw that wedding dress." One gray-flecked eyebrow lifted. "It was white. In my day a white dress meant something."

"Everybody wears white now, Dad." The fact that it actually *had* meant something in Casey's case didn't really have to be discussed. Did it?

"True." The older man sighed. "I guess it would be pretty rare these days to find a woman who'd saved herself for marriage. Of course, it'd probably be just as rare to find a man willing to go along with that decision."

Jake shifted uncomfortably. Casey had waited. Only to have her bridegroom jilt her at the altar. Though this might not be the best time to say that perhaps Casey might have mentioned that she was a virgin. It would only sound as if he was trying to duck responsibility. Hell, it even felt like that to him, and he knew it wasn't true. But whatever he said, judging by the look in his father's eyes, this wasn't going to be an easy conversation.

Just a few days ago the Parrish family had celebrated Thanksgiving. If he had known then what would be happening soon, Jake might have been a little less thankful.

Now, though, he was trying to be reasonable. A man of the nineties.

"Dad, Casey's a big girl. She makes her own decisions."

"So do you," Frank countered. "The right ones, I hope."

What did that mean? Oh, hell, he knew what it meant. No, he hadn't used any protection until after the barn door was open and the horse was frolicking. And all right, yes, there was a chance that Casey could be pregnant because of him. A *slim* chance.

Grumbling under his breath, Jake shifted his gaze to the snow-covered meadow beyond the ranch yard. Ridiculous. He might become a father because of a storm and a lost calf. He leaned his forearms on the top rail of the corral fence and tried to convince himself that there was nothing to worry about.

Frank Parrish sighed again, planted one elbow on the same fence rail and cupped his chin in his hand. "You know that Emma's going to be flapping her gums the minute she gets a clear path to a telephone."

"Yeah." But what did that really matter, Jake thought. He and Casey were two consenting single adults.

"And the fact that Casey ran out of the church and straight into your bed is going to make the tale interesting to a lot of folks."

Jake had a feeling he knew where this was going. He just didn't know how to stop it.

"Your mother..." Frank said.

Uh-oh, his dad was pulling out the big guns.

"She was always real fond of Casey. Thought of her as a daughter."

Hell, he refused to look on this little episode as incest! "She's not, though, remember?"

"As close as she can come without being blood."

True. As a girl, Casey *had* spent a lot of time at the ranch. His parents *had* doted on her. But she was all grown-up now. She didn't need a champion.

"That girl," Frank went on, "is like a part of this family. I won't have her cheaply used any more than I would stand by and watch some man take advantage of your sister."

Frank's mouth thinned into a grim line, and pain flickered briefly in his dark eyes. Jake knew he was thinking about Annie's useless ex-husband. There hadn't been anything either of them could do to protect Annie from hurt and embarrassment then. Obviously Frank was prepared to make up for that with Casey.

Jake stretched his neck as if he could feel a bow tie tightening around it. Across his shoulders, it was as if the snug fit of a rented tuxedo was already boxing him in.

"There's one way to take the sting out of Emma's gossip-spewing." Frank paused before continuing.

Jake knew what was coming. Blankly he studied the puff of his own breath as it misted in the cold air. He kept himself from speaking because he didn't want to prod his father into saying the words out loud.

He should have known that wouldn't stop him.

"You two can get married."

There it was. Tossed into the open where everyone could stare at it. The imaginary bow tie was strangling him now.

"Married?" Jake pushed away from the fence and shoved both hands into his coat pockets. He swiveled his head to stare at his father's calm determined features. "No thanks, Dad. I tried that once."

Frank didn't say a word. He just looked at his son.

Jake shifted uncomfortably. He hadn't seen that particular flare of disappointment in his father's eyes since the night of his seventeenth birthday. Like other teenage fools before him, he'd been convinced that a celebration without beer wasn't a celebration at all. Unfortunately, after his surprise party, he'd tried to drive himself home. He never saw the tree that jumped out into the road and bit his right fender. All he remembered to this day was the look on his father's face when he'd shown up at the police station to pick him up.

Jake had done everything he could since then to avoid reliving that particular sensation.

Until today.

Uneasily he glanced at the house again. Hell, maybe his father was right. Maybe he *should* ask Casey to marry him. It might be the nineties everywhere else in the country, but as for morality in small-town America, it was generally more like the nineties of the past century. And that wasn't altogether a bad thing. Until it affected him personally.

Still, there was something else to consider. Casey

would no doubt turn his proposal down, anyway. So he could do the right thing, avoid shaming himself in his father's eyes and still not worry about embarking on yet another disappointing marriage.

"Well?" Frank asked.

"I'll talk to her." Before he could change his mind, Jake started for the house.

Casey stood in front of the dresser and ran a brush through her tangled blond hair. Then, in the mirror above the heavy chest of drawers, she glanced wryly at the clothes she'd been given to wear. Jake's oversize sweats hung on her small frame. The ribbed cuffs fell past her wrists and had to be constantly pushed up. The pant legs could be pulled over her feet to serve as slippers.

A real femme fatale.

"What on earth went on yesterday?" Annie plopped down on Jake's bed and sat with her legs crossed.

Casey glanced at her friend in the mirror and lifted both eyebrows.

Annie laughed and held up one hand. "OK, I know what went on. What I can't figure out is *why*."

"I suppose it would really look bad for me if I said I didn't know."

"Look, Case." Annie leaned forward, elbows on her knees. "The last time we talked, you were practically walking down the aisle with—" she paused and pushed the end of her nose up with the tip of one finger "—Steven."

"Yeah, well," Casey said, "I was walking and Steven was running. In the other direction."

"Omigod. Jilted? The bastard *jilted* you?"

"Have you ever noticed what a lovely word that is? Jilted, I mean."

"Lovely?" Annie cocked her head and her long black hair, freed from its knot, swung to one side.

Casey turned around and leaned her fanny against the edge of the dresser. Watching her friend's confused face, she couldn't really blame her. *She* should be confused, too. Strangely enough, though, she wasn't.

It was as if she'd been released from prison to find herself in a wide glorious new world. All right. Steven *was* a nice enough guy, and maybe prison was too strong a word. But when she thought about the quick passionless kisses she and her ex-fiancé had shared and then compared them with Jake's kisses...well, there *was* no comparison.

The day before, she had almost married the wrong man for all the wrong reasons. To please her family. To avoid hurting Steven's feelings. And because canceling the wedding after all the time and money spent on it would have been unthinkable for her.

Today, however, it seemed *anything* was possible. Despite the embarrassment of being caught naked in Jake's bed by his father, of all people.

"I'll never be able to look your dad in the face again."

"I don't think anyone was looking at your face, Casey."

"Oh, God."

Annie chuckled again, got off the bed and walked over to her. "Don't worry about it."

"But your uncle Harry is a *minister*."

"Ministers have sex, I'm told." She paused and

shuddered. "Though the idea of him and Emma together is enough to make me want to take the veil."

Casey laughed and immediately felt better.

"See? Nothing's so bad it can't be cured with a good laugh."

"Hope you feel the same way when you see what Lisa's done to her pretty new dress."

Both women turned to look at Jake, standing in the doorway.

"What's she gotten into?" Annie sounded tired but resigned.

"Can't be sure," he said with a shrug. "But it's black and it looks permanent."

"Ohhh…!" Annie got to her feet. "I'll be back, Case. Don't go anywhere."

"She won't," Jake said.

Casey looked from her friend's retreating form to the cool steadiness of Jake's eyes. "I won't?"

"Not until we talk."

"About what?"

"Our wedding."

The room tilted and Casey grabbed hold of the dresser behind her to keep from sliding out the window.

Jake pried one of her hands free and dragged her over to the bed.

"Married?" She shook her head, then raised her confused eyes to meet his.

"Casey," he said, "Emma's in the kitchen inching closer to the phone every second. Harry and Dad won't be able to hold her down much longer."

"So?"

"So, with that phone in her hand, she's more potent than those tabloids in the grocery stores."

"Gossip bothers you?" Even as she asked it, Casey winced. From the little Annie had told her of Jake's divorce, it hadn't been pretty. No doubt the gossips had chewed on him for months.

"It's not me they'll be talking about this time." Jake started pacing. "I'm old news. But you—" he pointed at her "—are fresh meat."

"Oh."

Casey's big green eyes were fixed on him. His navy blue sweats shouldn't have looked so damn good on her. She was practically swimming in them and still she looked beautiful. He gritted his teeth and ignored the sudden rush of blood to his groin. She chewed her bottom lip. Her delicate features made her appear too fragile to stand up to the tidal wave of gossip and innuendo headed their way. Even though rationally he knew Casey was no spun-glass woman, he couldn't deny the protective urge rising in him.

"Jake, I don't live here anymore. Why should it matter what the people in Simpson say about me?"

"Morgan Hill isn't that far away," he reminded her. "And the Oakes name is well-known."

At the mention of her family, she paled.

No wonder, he told himself. Her parents would not be pleased at being the center of gossip. Jake scowled and turned away. Why did he care? All he'd intended was to ask her to marry him. To do the right thing. Why was he standing here trying to convince her to say yes, when he was hoping she would say no?

That was it. No more. It wasn't his business. If Casey felt she could stand up to Emma and her cronies—not to mention her father, Henderson Oakes—that was up to her. He had done his best. He had offered her marriage.

Lord, he could hardly wait for this day to be over. He rubbed the back of his neck as if to loosen that imaginary bow tie. Hell, he hadn't even had the opportunity to tell his family about the land he'd finally managed to buy. This was supposed to be his big day. He should feel triumphant. Victorious.

Ah, well.

"All right, Jake," Casey said softly.

He turned around to look at her. "All right what?"

"All right, I'll marry you."

The bow tie was back. Strangling him.

Beauty and the Beast.

The phrase leaped into his mind as he watched his bride on her father's arm, moving sedately across the great room toward him. Casey looked beautiful. Her hair fell loose in shining waves beneath a crown of red roses and carnations. Soft filmy white cotton fluttered and swirled about her legs, and he had to admit that he liked this dress much better than the one she'd been wearing the week before.

His gaze shot to the Beast. Henderson Oakes. A man of little humor and even less patience. Grimly, as if under protest, he escorted his smiling daughter toward her groom.

In the front row of chairs Frank Parrish sat beside Emma, who continually dabbed a flowered hanky to dry eyes. On the other side of the makeshift aisle, Casey's mother, Hilary, was dressed to the teeth in raw silk and diamonds. She perched uncomfortably on her chair as if expecting the thing to collapse beneath her perfectly toned and sculpted body.

No wonder Casey hadn't wanted to call her parents until the night before the wedding. Hell, he wouldn't have blamed her if she hadn't called them at all. He even understood more clearly now why she had agreed to this marriage in the first place. Marrying him had to be better than having to listen to those two tell you what a disappointment you were.

Then the Beast was there. In front of him. He placed Beauty's hand in Jake's, then took a long step back, distancing himself from the union.

Tucking her hand in the crook of Jake's arm, Casey turned with him to face Uncle Harry, who was conducting the ceremony. The moment she touched Jake her insides settled down. She felt her parents' disapproving gazes driving into her back. But offsetting their grimness were the combined good wishes of everyone else gathered here at the ranch. And her brothers were on her side. Casey leaned forward and looked at the twin standing beside Jake. J.T. winked at her.

Grinning, she straightened again, glanced at Annie on her left, then focused on the minister.

Watery sunshine sifted through the tall front windows, and the scent of fresh pine drifted to them from the decorative boughs hung about the huge room. This small informal wedding, planned and thrown together in less than a week, was, to her mind, more beautiful than the "event" her mother's personal planner had spent four months staging.

A log in the fireplace snapped, and Casey moved closer to Jake. Odd how things worked out. Technically she should have been on a honeymoon in Hawaii with a different groom. Yet here she was marrying a man she'd loved since childhood, despite the fact that he was a reluctant groom.

"I do," Jake said, and his deep voice rumbled through her. Casey blinked and brought her wandering attention back to the business at hand just in time to promise to "love, honor and cherish."

"I now pronounce you husband and wife." Uncle Harry smiled benevolently. "You may kiss your bride, Jake."

He turned obediently to Casey and looked down into green eyes that held far too much optimism. A flicker of regret sputtered to life inside him, then faded again. He had already learned the hard way what marriage was like. It was a shame that he would have to be on hand to watch Casey's education. Almost made a man wish he actually believed in happily-ever-after.

A smattering of applause rose up from their small select audience, demanding the wedding kiss. The light in Casey's eyes had dimmed a bit, and he knew it was his fault for hesitating. Dipping his head, he bent to claim the obligatory kiss. The moment his lips brushed hers, though, obligation flew out of his mind. She leaned into him, tipping her head back. His arms closed around her and he deepened the kiss, parting her lips with a thrust of his tongue. Something fluttered into life in his chest. His blood roared through his veins. Electricity hummed between them. She wrapped her arms around his neck and clung to him. Her tongue met his in a silent dance of promise, and his body's response was staggering.

Absently he heard people cheering and above the raised voices, a wild whistle that had to have come from one of the twins. Lifting his head again, he stared down at his wife and heard his uncle Harry say, "Guess there's no denying this is a love match!"

Love, he wasn't willing to bet on, Jake thought.

But lust, at least, was honest.

"Be honest, Cassandra," her father said. "You participated in this…marriage as a way of saving face. Steven humiliated us and you thought to assuage that somehow."

She swallowed and looked through the doorway into the great room. Everyone seemed to be having a good time. She wished desperately she was out there with them, not standing in the kitchen listening to the lecture she'd known was coming.

"How you could believe that marrying a man you hardly know within a week of being—" her mother lowered her voice, "—jilted would erase public humiliation, I have no idea."

"I've known Jake for years, Mother."

Hilary's eyebrows drew together before she apparently remembered that frowning caused ugly lines. Her features resettled into a familiar expressionless mask.

"Of course, you've known the family. But really, Cassandra, one doesn't simply put aside one fiancé and snatch up another as if they were apples in a barrel."

Casey inhaled deeply.

"I'm certain young Steven would have come to his senses shortly." Her father's voice sliced at her. "There was no need for you to panic."

"I didn't panic," she said firmly. "And even if Steven had come back, I wouldn't have married him."

"Of course you would, dear. Simple misunderstandings are no reason to throw away a perfectly good future. These things happen between couples." Her mother waved a silk handkerchief scented with designer perfume to make her point.

Simple misunderstanding? Being left at the altar in front of a few hundred people could hardly be called a simple misunderstanding.

"I've already spoken to Steven's father. He's going to straighten out that son of his and then things will be as they should. As soon as we take care of this marriage of yours, Cassandra," her father said briskly. "Which wouldn't have been necessary if you'd bothered to tell us of your plans *before* last night."

That was precisely *why* she hadn't told her parents about her wedding until the night before. In fact, if Jake hadn't insisted, she wouldn't have told them at all until well after the ceremony.

And how typical of Henderson Oakes to attend the wedding and give the bride away, all the while trying to figure out ways of ending the marriage. She'd never doubted that her parents would show up of course. Above all, Henderson and Hilary were concerned with the *appearance* of things. They'd always held the opinion that as long as they looked like a happy family, they were.

"Father," she said, determined to make him listen, "I'm married to Jake now. And that's how it's going to stay."

"Nonsense."

Nothing had changed. But then, why had she expected it to? They never listened. They never heard her. Casey wanted to run into the other room, where dance music issued from the stereo. She wanted to lose herself among the laughing, smiling, dancing people. Distance herself from the people who should have loved her most.

"Casey dear, divorce is simply a part of life." Hilary Oakes waved her hanky again. "Why in even the best of families, divorce has become... commonplace."

"I'll have my accountant contact Mr. Parrish," Henderson said. "I'm sure we can work out a reasonable solution to this and compensate him for any inconvenience."

Casey's fingernails dug into her palms. She concentrated on the physical pain because it was so much easier to bear than her parents' dismissive words. *Inconvenience*. She couldn't help wondering if Jake thought of her as an inconvenience, too.

"Casey?"

She spun around to look at her husband as he

walked toward them. Never had she been so glad to see him. He looked wonderful in his tuxedo, even though she knew he hated getting what he called "duded up."

He nodded briefly to her mother, then held out his hand to her father. Reluctantly, it seemed, Henderson Oakes shook his new son-in-law's hand. He opened his mouth to speak, but Jake forestalled him, turning, instead, to Casey. He took both her hands in his and gave them a gentle squeeze. "I came to claim our first dance, Mrs. Parrish."

She blinked, swallowed and blinked again.

It must be the overhead lighting. Making her see things in his eyes that she wanted to see. Concern. Genuine caring. Perhaps just a hint of love.

But it didn't matter, anyway. Whatever the reason he had come, she was grateful for the rescue.

"I'd be delighted, Mr. Parrish."

Seven

"**I** moved my things into the spare room," Jake said, and somehow managed to avoid her eyes.

"I don't understand."

Neither did he, completely. All he knew for sure was that vows alone didn't make a marriage. For that, you needed love. He'd learned that the hard way.

Their guests were gone. The few leftovers had been stored in the refrigerator. Most of the mess had been cleaned up. Jake and Casey had been left alone.

And the house was quiet.

Intimate.

"Look, Casey," he said, and shifted his gaze to meet hers now. Anything less would be too cowardly. "We both know this isn't an ordinary marriage."

"It could be."

One of the roses in her crown had slipped loose of its wire and was lying along the line of her cheek. Her face was flushed with soft color, and near her right breast were raspberry stains in the shape of tiny fingerprints. Apparently Lisa had claimed a dance or two with her new aunt and hadn't bothered to wash her hands first.

Raspberries and Casey's breasts. An intriguing combination.

He stiffened, but ignored the stirrings in his body. He'd be damned if he was going to be led around by his hormones.

"Casey," he said, his voice thick, "let's just see how it goes, huh? Give each other a little room here. Get used to each other."

She cocked her head and he refused to acknowledge the way her soft sweet-smelling hair lay across her throat.

"Why did you ask me to marry you?"

He frowned. "Lots of reasons."

"Give me one," she said, and crossed her arms under her breasts.

Jake's gaze slipped, and before he caught himself and looked away, he thought he saw the dark pink tips of her nipples pressing against the fabric of her gown. How in the hell such a modest dress could suddenly seem so enticing was beyond him.

"Fine," he grumbled. "You might be pregnant."

"Not good enough," she countered. "We'll know for sure about that in a week or two. You could have waited."